~∞~ The Classic Tale of ~∞~
Squirrel Nutkin

Louis Weber, C.E.O.
Publications International, Ltd.
7373 North Cicero Avenue
Lincolnwood, Illinois 60646

Based on the original story by Beatrix Potter

Manufactured in U.S.A.

8 7 6 5 4 3 2 1

ISBN 1-56173-476-4

Cover illustration by Anita Nelson

Book illustrations by Pat Schoonover

This is a tale about a tail—a tail that belonged to a little red squirrel named Nutkin. Squirrel Nutkin had a brother called Twinkleberry. He had a great many cousins, too. They all lived in the woods at the edge of a lake.

In the middle of the lake was an island covered with trees and nut bushes. Among the trees and bushes stood a hollow oak tree. It was the house of an owl called Old Brown.

One autumn day, when the nuts were ripe and the leaves on the bushes were golden, Nutkin, Twinkleberry, and all the other squirrels went to the edge of the lake.

They made little rafts out of twigs, and they paddled over the water to Owl Island to gather nuts. Each squirrel had a little sack and a little oar; they spread their tails for sails.

They also took with them three fat mice as a present for Old Brown. The squirrels put the mice on his doorstep. Twinkleberry and the other little squirrels bowed and said politely, "Old Mr. Brown, may we please have permission to gather nuts on your island?"

But Nutkin's manners were very rude. He bounced up and down like a little red *cherry*, singing—

"Riddle me, riddle me, rot-tot-tote!
A little wee man, in a red red coat!
A staff in his hand, and a stone in his
  throat;
If you tell me this riddle, I'll give you
  a groat."

Now, Mr. Brown was not interested in a groat, which is a coin. He paid no attention to Nutkin; he shut his eyes and went to sleep. The squirrels left Mr. Brown and filled their little sacks with nuts. They all sailed home in the evening.

The next morning the squirrels returned to the island with a fat mole for Old Brown. They laid it in the owl's doorway, and asked, "Mr. Brown, may we gather more nuts?"

But Nutkin, who had no respect, began to tickle the sleeping Mr. Brown with a twig.

Mr. Brown woke up suddenly and carried the mole into his house. He shut the door in Nutkin's face. Soon a little thread of blue *smoke* from a wood fire came up from the top of the tree. Nutkin peeked through the keyhole and sang—

"A house full, a hole full!
And you cannot gather a bowl full!"

The squirrels gathered nuts from all over the island. But Nutkin gathered crab apples, and sat on a stump watching the door of Old Brown.

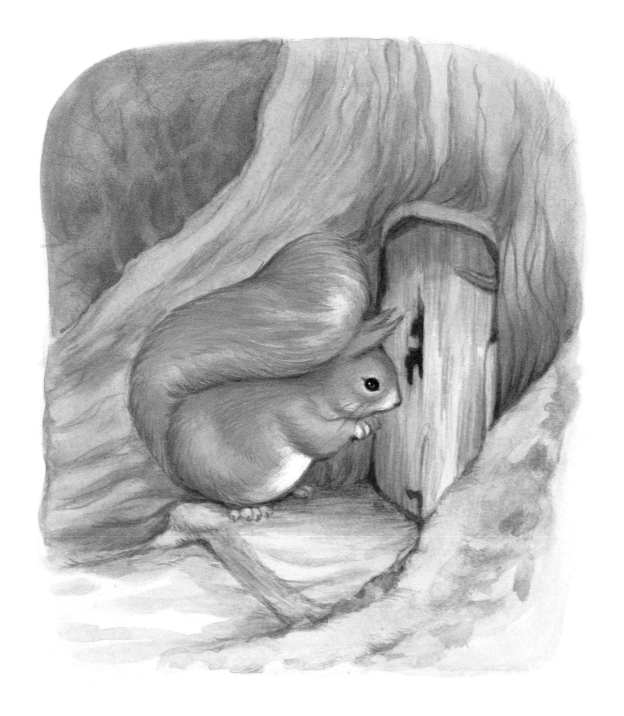

On the third day the squirrels went fishing very early. They caught seven fat minnows for Old Brown and paddled over the lake to Owl Island.

Twinkleberry and six other squirrels each carried a minnow. But Nutkin, who did not have nice manners, brought no present at all. He ran in front, singing—

"The man in the wilderness said to me,
'How many strawberries grow in the sea?'
I answered him as I thought good—
'As many red herrings as grow in the wood.'"

But Mr. Brown was not interested in riddles—not even when the answer was given to him.

The squirrels filled their sacks with nuts. But Nutkin played a bowling game with crab apples and pinecones.

On the fourth day the squirrels went to Owl Island for the last time. They brought an *egg* as a good-bye present for Old Brown. But Nutkin ran in front laughing and shouting—

"Humpty Dumpty lies in the beck,
With a white counterpane round his neck,
Forty doctors and forty wrights,
Cannot put Humpty Dumpty to rights!"

Now Mr. Brown liked eggs. He opened one eye and shut it again. But he still did not speak.

Then Nutkin became very rude—

"Old Mr. B! Old Mr. B!
Hickamore, Hackamore, on the King's
    kitchen door;
All the King's horses, and all the King's
    men,
Couldn't drive Hickamore, Hackamore,
Off the King's kitchen door."

Nutkin danced about like a *sunbeam*. But still Old Brown said nothing at all.

Nutkin took a running jump right onto the head of Old Brown!

All at once there was a fluttering and a scuffling and a loud "Squeak!"

The other squirrels scampered away into the bushes. And when they came back very cautiously, peeking around the tree, there was Old Brown sitting on his doorstep. He sat quite still, with his eyes closed, as if nothing had happened.

But Nutkin was in his coat pocket!

This looks like the end of the story, but it isn't.

Old Brown carried Nutkin into his house, and held him up by the tail, intending to eat him. But Nutkin struggled so very hard that his tail broke in two. He dashed up the stairs and escaped out of the attic window!

And to this day, if you meet Squirrel Nutkin and ask him a riddle, he will throw sticks at you, stamp his feet, scold, and shout, *"Cuck-cuck-cuck-cur-r-r-cuck-k-k!"*